For my grandma, Mabel Owen,
who never learned to drive
but was always going somewhere—F. G.

For my niece, Allyson Harris.
I can't wait to see
the places you go!—A. B.

BEACH LANE BOOKS • An imprint of Simon & Schuster Children's Publishing Division • 1230 Avenue of the Americas, New York, New York 10020 • Text copyright © 2019 by Frances Gilbert • Illustrations copyright © 2019 by Allison Black • All rights reserved, including the right of reproduction in whole or in part in any form. • BEACH LANE BOOKS is a trademark of Simon & Schuster, Inc. • For information about special discounts for bulk purchases, please contact Simon & Schuster Special Sales at 1-866-506-1949 or business@simonandschuster.com. • The Simon & Schuster Speakers Bureau can bring authors to your live event. For more information or to book an event, contact the Simon & Schuster Speakers Bureau at 1-866-248-3049 or visit our website at www .simonspeakers.com. • Book design by Lauren Rille • The text for this book was set in Ariel Rounded. • The illustrations for this book were rendered in Adobe Photoshop. • Manufactured in China • 0120 SCP • 10 9 8 7 6 5 4 3 2 • Library of Congress Cataloging-in-Publication Data • Names: Gilbert, Frances, 1969– author. | Black, Allison, 1986– illustrator. • Title: Go, girls, go! / Frances Gilbert ; illustrated by Allison Black. • Description: First edition. | New York : Beach Lane Books, [2019] | Summary: Illustrations and easy-to-read, rhyming text celebrate girls who race, fly, and drive everything from a dump truck to a rocket ship. • Identifiers: LCCN 2019000746 | ISBN 9781534424821 (hardcover : alk. paper) | ISBN 9781534424838 (eBook) • Subjects: | CYAC: Stories in rhyme. | Motor vehicle driving—Fiction. | Vehicles—Fiction. | Sex role—Fiction. • Classification: LCC PZ8.3.G384 Go 2019 | DDC [E]—dc23 LC record available at https://lccn.loc.gov/2019000746

GO, GIRLS, GO!

written by
Frances Gilbert

illustrated by
Allison Black

Beach Lane Books • New York London Toronto Sydney New Delhi

Emma drives a fire engine,

Meg conducts a train,

Jayla steers a big red tractor
hauling loads of grain.

VROOM!

goes Emma.

CLANK!

goes Jayla.

HOOT!

goes Meg.

Kelly speeds an ambulance,

Ella revs her tow truck,

Sarah's tugboat saves the day
whenever ships are stuck.

WOOO!

goes Kelly.

TOOT!

goes Sarah.

WHIRR! goes Ella.

Ruby's in her taxicab,

Bessie flies a plane,

Rachel builds a city tower
with her giant crane.

Whoosh!
goes Bessie.

GIRLS,

GO!

Mia's on a motorcycle,

Rana loves her jeep,

Daisy's dump truck loads up rubble in a giant heap.

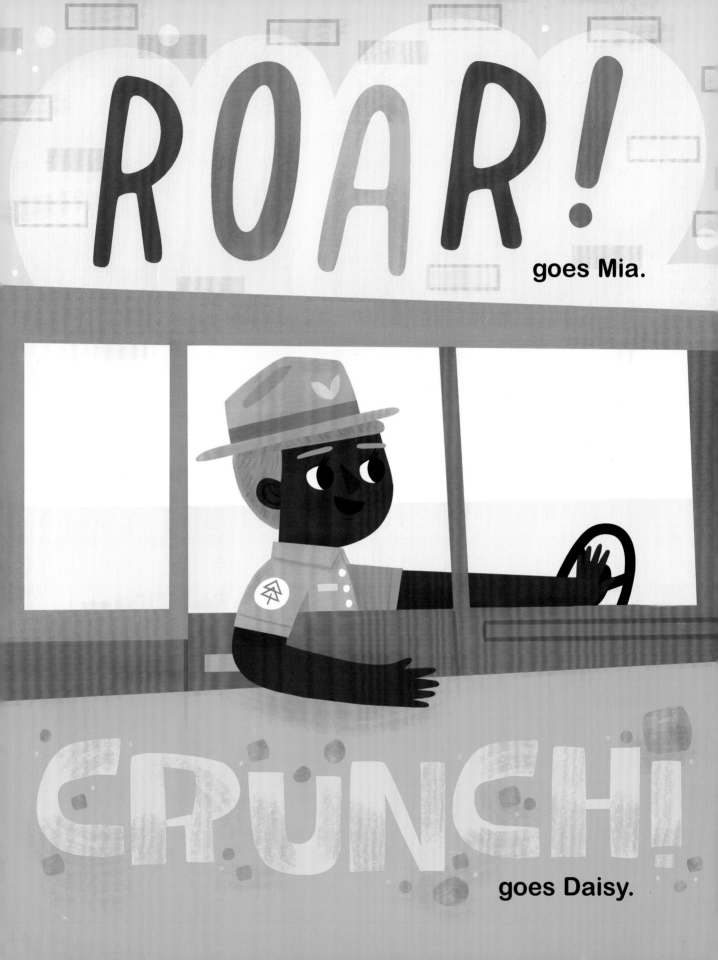

ROAR! goes Mia.

CRUNCH! goes Daisy.

HONK!

goes Rana.

Girls can race . . .

and girls can fly.

Girls can rocket way up high.

What about you?

GIVE IT

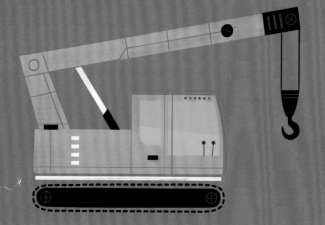

AMBULANCE

A TRY!

FIRE